The Last Laugh

Jose Aruego & Ariane Dewey

 Dial Books for Young Readers

DIAL BOOKS FOR YOUNG READERS
A division of Penguin Young Readers Group • Published by The Penguin Group
Penguin Group (USA) Inc., 375 Hudson Street, New York, NY 10014, U.S.A.

Penguin Group (Canada), 90 Eglinton Avenue East, Suite 700, Toronto, Ontario, Canada M4P
2Y3 (a division of Pearson Penguin Canada Inc. • Penguin Books Ltd, 80 Strand, London
WC2R 0RL, England • Penguin Ireland, 25 St. Stephen's Green, Dublin 2, Ireland (a division of
Penguin Books Ltd) • Penguin Group (Australia), 250 Camberwell Road, Camberwell, Victoria
3124, Australia (a division of Pearson Australia Group Pty Ltd) • Penguin Books India Pvt Ltd,
11 Community Centre, Panchsheel Park, New Delhi - 110 017, India • Penguin Group (NZ),
Cnr Airborne and Rosedale Roads, Albany, Auckland 1310, New Zealand (a division of Pearson
New Zealand Ltd) • Penguin Books (South Africa) (Pty) Ltd, 24 Sturdee Avenue, Rosebank,
Johannesburg 2196, South Africa • Penguin Books Ltd, Registered Offices: 80 Strand, London
WC2R 0RL, England

The publisher does not have any control over and does not assume any responsibility
for author or third-party websites or their content.
Manufactured in China on acid-free paper
10 9 8 7 6 5 4 3 2 1

Library of Congress Cataloging-in-Publication Data
Aruego, Jose.
The last laugh / Jose Aruego and Ariane Dewey.
p. cm.
Summary: A wordless tale in which a clever duck outwits a bullying snake.
ISBN 0-8037-3093-4
[1. Snakes—Fiction. 2. Ducks—Fiction. 3. Bullies—Fiction.
4. Stories without words.] I. Dewey, Ariane. II. Title.
PZ7.A7475 2006   [E]—dc22   2005048461

The art was prepared using pen-and-ink and gouache.

To my calligraphy teacher, Reggie Ezell (hiss!)—J.A.

HISS!

HEE...
HEE...

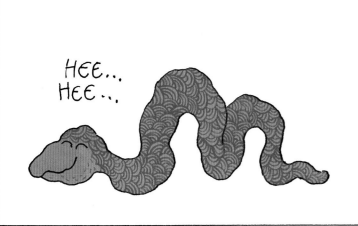

HEE...
HEE...

QUACK! QUACK!

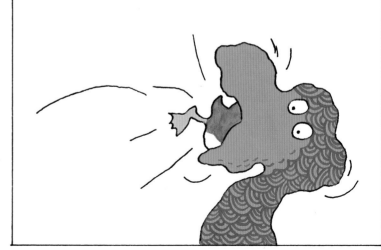

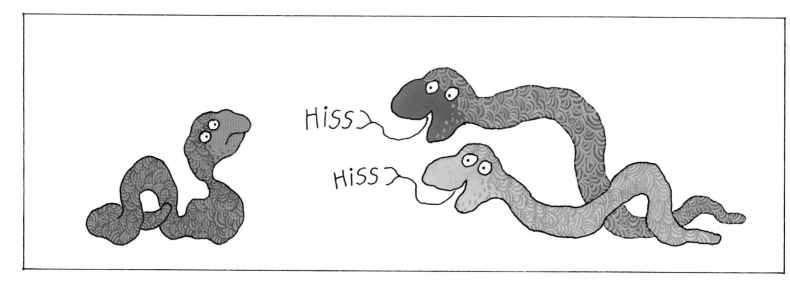

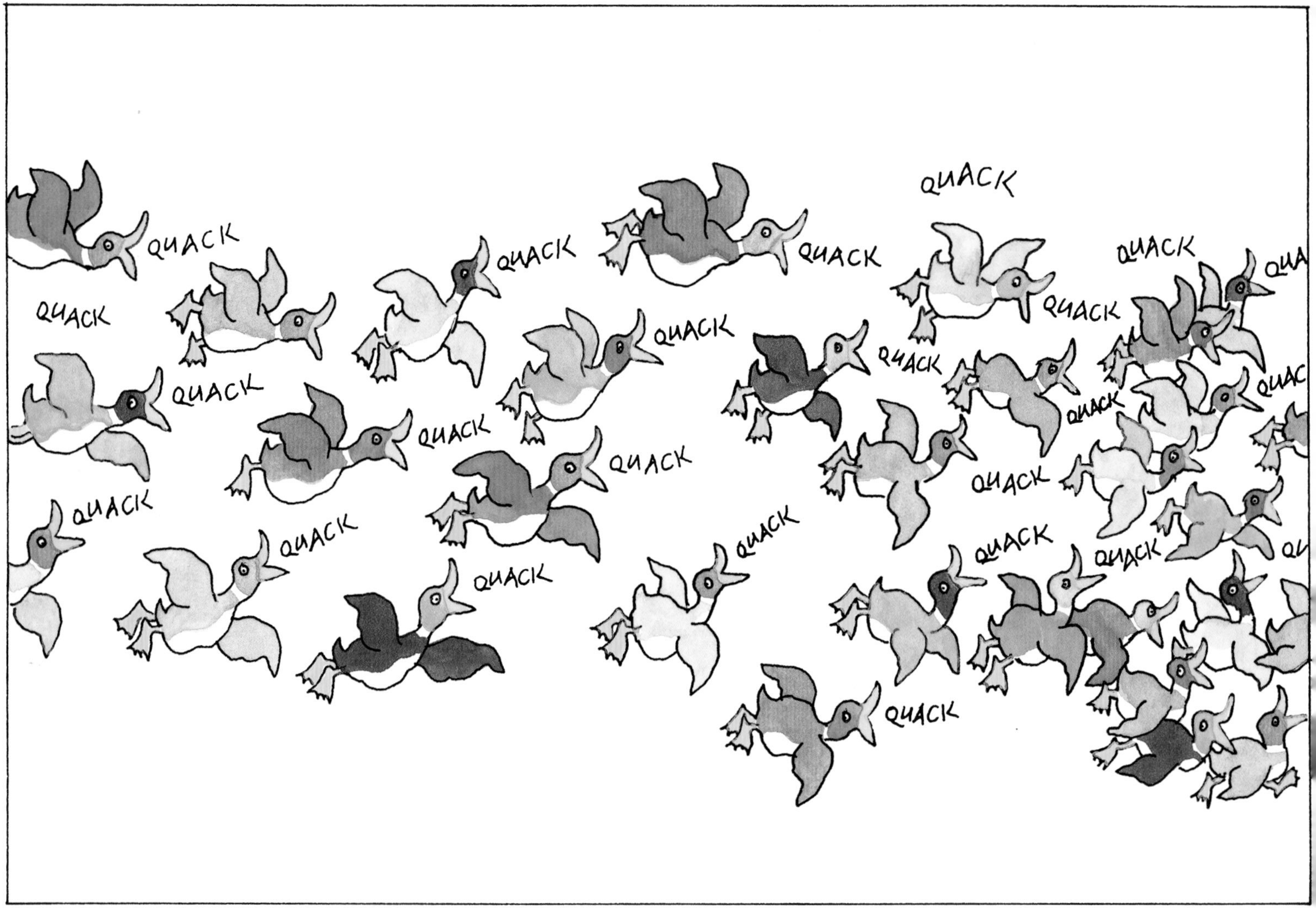
QUACK
QUACK
QUACK
QUACK
QUACK
QUACK
QUACK
QUACK
QUACK
QUACK
QUACK
QUACK
QUACK
QUACK
QUACK
QUACK
QUACK
QUACK
QUACK
QUACK
QUACK

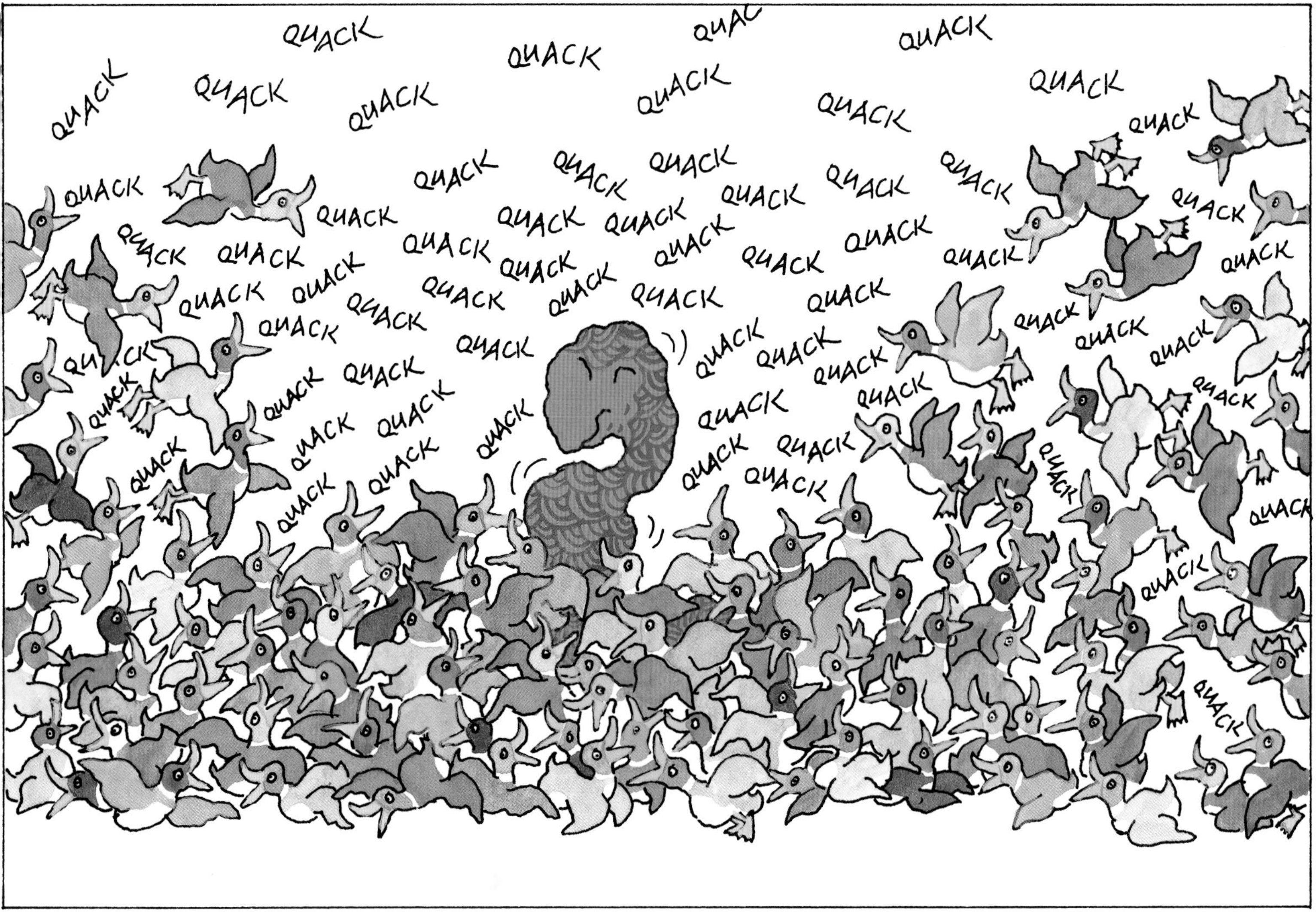

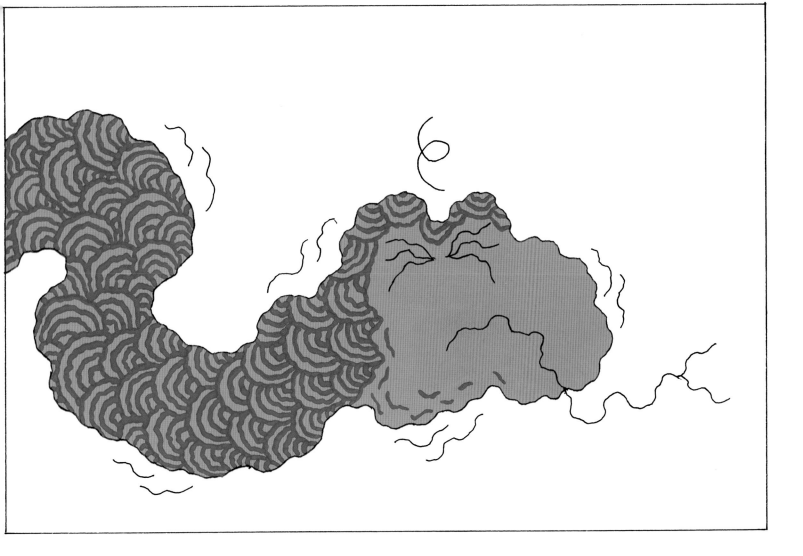

THIS BOOK IS DEDICATED TO BULLIES EVERYWHERE

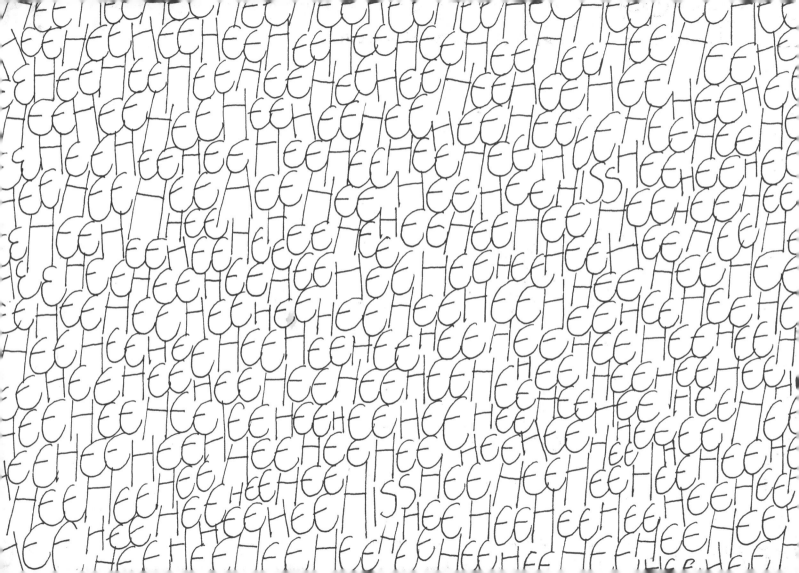